Oh, Sir Bragalot!

NEW FRONTIER PUBLISHING

To Neve and Alex,
always – S D

First published in Great Britain 2021
by New Frontier Publishing Europe Ltd
Uncommon, 126 New King's Road, London, SW6 4LZ
www.newfrontierpublishing.co.uk

A CIP catalogue record for this book is
available from the British Library.

ISBN: 978-1-913639-64-8

Designed by Verity Clark

Printed and bound in China
1 3 5 7 9 10 8 6 4 2

OH, Sir Bragalot!

BY SHARON DAVEY

Meet **Sir Bragalot**, a **Knight** of the Round Table and an all-round, terrible **bragger** ...

He tells **unbelievable** tales!

'I'm great, I'm fantastic,
don't you wish you were **ME**?!'

'I can jump **higher**
than you!'

'Look at me! I can run **faster** than you!'

'I'm **stronger** than YOU!'

Oh, Sir Bragalot!

This went on for a LONG TIME. The other knights had heard all of his brags and boasts before – and they were bored, **bored**, **bored**!

One afternoon, when Sir Hector returned from a dangerous quest in a faraway land, King Arthur awarded him the Cross of Bravery.

Sir Bragalot didn't like
other knights getting medals
and trophies that *he* didn't have.

'I'm so much **BRAVER** than him!' boasted Sir Bragalot.

'I'm SO brave I could go on an even
BIGGER quest!' he bragged.

'In fact, I am the **BRAVEST** knight in the whole world!' he shouted to everybody.

Oh, Sir Bragalot!

The knights were very happy to give Sir Bragalot this chance.

'Well, how about it, Sir Bragalot?'

'You are the **biggest**, **strongest** and **bravest** of us all!'

'*I am?*' said Sir Bragalot. 'I mean … er … **YES**, **I am**!'

Sir Bragalot set off on his noble quest with his knees knocking and his lips wobbling.

Sir Bragalot panicked. Bragging would *not* help him here.

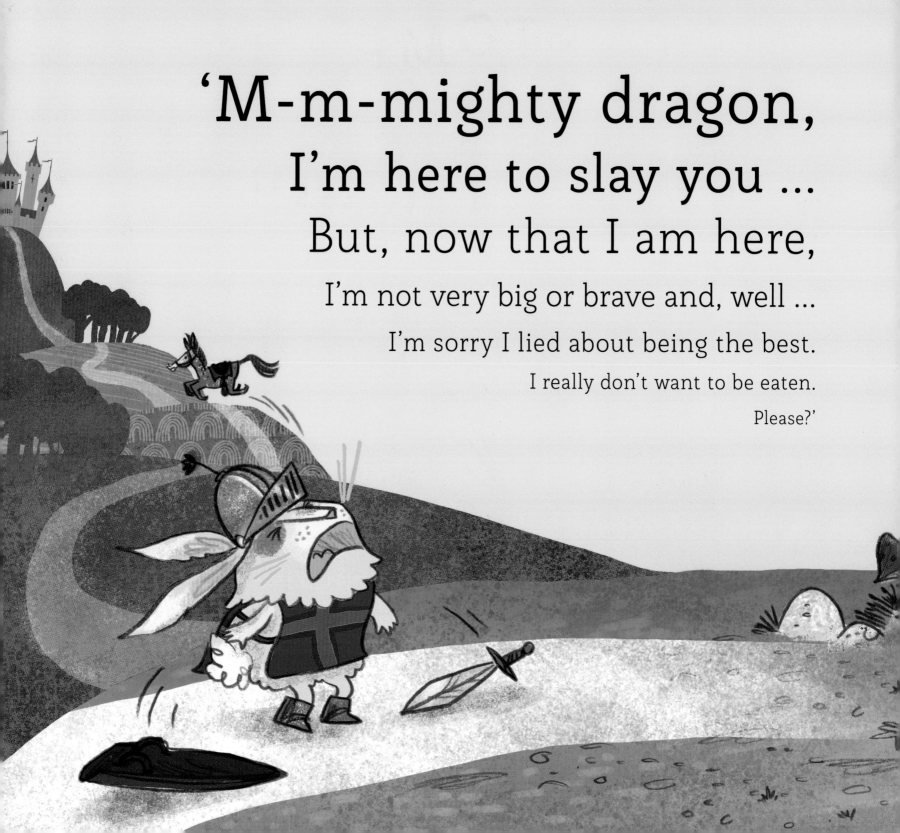

'M-m-mighty dragon,
I'm here to slay you ...
But, now that I am here,
I'm not very big or brave and, well ...
I'm sorry I lied about being the best.
I really don't want to be eaten.
Please?'

STOMP,

STOMP,

STOMP ...

Then out of the cave came ...

... the teeniest, tiniest dragon you have ever seen.

'Why, you're so **SMALL**!'
Sir Bragalot squealed joyfully.

'You're tiny, you're teeny,
you're mini, you're weeny!'

Uh-oh. Here he goes again ...

... well, almost never.

'Did I ever tell you about the time I defeated
a really **gigantic**, **super-enormous**, **dangerous**
dragon? Once upon a time ...'